THE FAITH OF THE TOWN FOOL

A CHRISTIAN NOVELETTE

BY

PAUL JOHNSTON SR.

CHAPTER ONE
MEET SHEEP

There wasn't much at Andrew's Crossing other than two roads that crossed one another, a few dilapidated old houses, an elementary school, an abandoned church, and a strange six sided corner grocery building with five porches that went almost all the way around the building. There were rocking chairs on all the porches where the locals could come and sit and gossip and spend their money at the store. The store was a long, narrow, building that would without doubt catch the attention of any stranger who happened to pass by the Crossing because of its strange shape. Equally strange was the name on the building, "Sheep's Market".

Clarence Andrews was the proprietor, but he had picked up the nickname "Sheep" as a youngster. Miss Mabel Young, who had taught at the local school for more than fifty years, had accidentally given him his nickname that stuck for a lifetime during a moment of frustration. She said, "Clarence, I swear boy, your mother should have named you 'Sheep' because, I swear child, you are always Baa-d". The other children all laughed hysterically at their teacher's rare attempt at humor and for that matter so did Clarence. It wasn't that he was a mean child, he was simply what later educators would call hyperactive. His mind was always darting off one direction or the other getting him into trouble, but he had a good heart and was well liked by the other children in spite of the fact that he usually wound up standing in the corner or wearing a dunce hat at least some portion of every day. One of those other children who laughed that day was his long time friend, Dr. Grover Grant.

This day found Dr. Grant approaching the store to speak with his old friend, Sheep. As he walked up on the porch, a tear rolled down his face. Sheep met him at the door. "Hey Doc, I didn't think I'd have to see your ugly face again 'til Thursday."
"Well, that was my plan, but I figured I had better stop by. Can we go back into your place and talk privately?"
"Sure, I'll have Millie run over from next door and watch the store for me." "Will, run over and get Millie to watch the store for

me."

Will responded in a halting stammering cadence, "Okay, Daddy."

Sheep watched as his seventeen year old son awkwardly tried to run next door. Will was severely afflicted with cerebral palsy. Both his speech and muscle coordination were affected.

As soon as Millie arrived, the two old friends went back into the residence. At one end of the rectangular shaped market was a triangular shaped addition containing a living room, dining area, and kitchen. At the other end of the store was a triangular shaped living area with a bathroom and two bedrooms. The storeroom and the two adjacent living quarters filled out the six sided building. Only the back wall of the market didn't have an adjacent porch where customers could sit and socialize.

Sheep motioned to Doc to have a seat. Then they sat down.

"Doc, Somehow I get the feelin' that this ain't no social call."

"Well Sheep, I reckon you know me pretty well by now. I hate like everything to have to tell you what I've got to tell you. I just couldn't bring myself to tell you what I believed was happening when you were in my office the other day. In the mean time, I've tried to read as much as I could on the subject from the latest medical journals and I even called up a couple doctors that I figured were a little smarter than me, but nothing has changed from what I originally thought so now I got to tell you what I don't want to."

"Well Doc, just spit it out. I reckon I already know what it is you need to tell me."

"Sheep, you're dying and there's not one earthly thing I as your doctor can do about it. You need to get your affairs in order and prepare to meet your Maker."

"Well, I reckon we all commence to dyin' little by little the day we're born. How much time do I have?"

"Only the good Lord knows that one for sure, but I'd say if you don't over exert that weak heart of yours, you probably can make it another six months. Maybe a year if you don't exert yourself too much and don't get too stressed out over anything."

"That's a lot easier said than done given the conditions in the country about now. I know that Mr. Hoover says that prosperity is just around the corner, but I have a feelin' that Mr. Hoover is goin' to get kicked out of his big White House come November just like so many other people have been in the last couple years. I've had to let my stock boy go to try to save on expenses. So I've got to handle all the stock myself and as for stress, I'm a rich man on paper, but I really don't know how much longer I can afford to keep the doors of this store open. Everybody wants a little more credit and few are paying me in cash. It's a struggle to replenish my stock let alone meet my own expenses. None of the farmers have made any money since before 1930. This drought has about starved them all out. I don't even remember the last time it rained around here."

"Well, all I can say is to try to do the best you can not to overdo yourself or get too upset. We're all struggling just to make ends meet."

"Honestly Doc, if it weren't for Will, the thought of dyin' wouldn't be all that disturbin' to me. I'd welcome the opportunity to see my Mary again. I've known heaven is my home ever since that day that Mary talked me into goin' to church with her and

the Lord got a hold of my heart. I trusted
Jesus as my Savior and I reckon if I can trust
him with my life, I can trust him with my
death. I just don't know what will become of
my poor little Will."
"You know I'll watch out for him as much as
I can."
"I know Doc, and you don't know how much
I appreciate that and I know that when I'm
gone, Millie will keep her eye on him as
well, but that boy needs his dad."
"That's a tough one for sure. You know that
you'll have to sit him down and tell him. You
can't just put it off till you keel over. That
wouldn't be right or fair to him."
"I know Doc, I just dread doin' it."

CHAPTER TWO
WILL

Will had arrived into this world under the worst of circumstances. The umbilical cord was wrapped around his neck three times and in the process of being born, precious oxygen had been shut off to his brain through strangulation. The resulting brain damage he sustained affected both his speech and his mobility and left him slightly intellectually challenged as well. He was not nearly as challenged though as his cruel schoolmates assumed. To make matters worse, Will's mother died trying to bring him into the world. Doc had been away on an emergency when Mary went into labor and the midwife was simply not as well trained as an experienced doctor to deal with the difficult delivery. Mary knew she was dying and made Sheep swear to her to raise her child in the fear and admonition of the Lord and to honor her memory by not growing bitter, but by drawing up close to the Lord and living a dedicated Christian life. Her grave was located behind the store between their garden and their orchard. Sheep often walked back to her grave to pour out his heart to her when life overwhelmed him. Sheep often felt lonely and with the exception of Doc Grant who was always busy helping someone, he had nobody else to confide in. He knew that Mary wasn't there in that grave, but it was just his way of dealing with the difficult times in life.

Keeping his promise to Mary was hard at times for Sheep, but he was a man of his word and he read the Bible to Will every night before they went to bed from his infancy. Will had a tender heart for the things of the Lord and Sheep loved his son and was proud of him in spite of his limitations. Will came to faith in Christ at an early age after one of their nightly Bible readings. Sheep had the privilege of introducing his son to his Heavenly Father. The Bible says that all those who will live godly lives will suffer persecution and Will's handicap did not buy him an exemption from that rule.

One time when Will was about twelve years old, Sheep noticed that for the last several nights Will had barely touched his food at suppertime. Later that night Sheep heard crying coming from the room next to his where Will slept.

"Son, I could hear you crying from in my room, please tell me what's wrong?"

"I can't tell you Daddy."

"Son, you know I love you and surely you also know that you can tell me anything."

"I know that Daddy, it's just that I don't want to make you sad. I do have something I really need to ask you though? Daddy, did I kill Mommy?"

"Oh no, Son. That's not true at all. What would make you ask such a question?"

"It was just something someone said to me at school."

"Won't you tell me what was said to you, Will?"

"I don't want to talk about it, Daddy."

"Okay, we won't then. Son don't worry about stupid stuff that people say to you. Just forget it and go to sleep. I love you son."

"I love you too, Daddy."

Sheep had tossed and turned all that night worrying about his son and what horrific things might have been said to him at school. He knew it would do no good to ask Will about it again because Will loved him and was afraid that what was said to him would hurt him. He decided to go to school and ask his teacher if she knew what was going on.

When Will headed out to school the next morning, Sheep left shortly afterwards and headed toward a stand of woods that ran next to the road that Will would have to take to get to school. Sheep walked just out of Will's sight through the woods parallel to the road. Given Will's physical limitations and slow pace, it didn't take long for Sheep to catch up to Will and to get a crystal clear picture of exactly what was happening. The snotty little McPherson twins came running up behind Will and intentionally knocked his books from his arm. Will didn't say a word to them. He just started scooping up his books from the ground using his good arm. Sheep was just about ready to come out of the woods when he heard the most cruel words that he had ever heard come out of the mouths of those two hooligans. In unison they said their filthy rhyme.

Mary had a little lamb.
He was such a little retard
He killed his mommy coming out
Now she's buried in their yard.

The usually calm Sheep clenched his fists. His face turned beet red. For a moment there, Sheep nearly reverted back to the man he had been before accepting the Lord. He said to himself, "If their parents won't teach those little brats how to behave, I'll sure be glad to teach them a lesson they will never forget." Providentially, before Sheep could move a muscle, God himself intervened by way of an enormous pigeon sitting on a branch right above the two boys. Let us say that nature called out to the pigeon at just the right moment and splat, it dumped its load right on the forehead of the worse of the two boys. Not only that, but it splashed right into his foul mouth. Afterwards, there were some words coming out of that boy's mouth that he really didn't want Will's ears hearing, but he was cussing so and trying to throw rocks at the pigeon so intently that Will walked on to school that morning in perfect peace and safety.

Later, Sheep went to school over the lunch break and asked to speak privately with the teacher. He explained how horribly Will had been treated on his way to school, but the teacher just shrugged and asked what she could do. She said that Will was different from the other children and it was to be expected that he would be treated differently by them.

"That's just life. Truly, Will doesn't belong here in school with the normal children."

"Well, that's the first sensible thing you've said. Will is coming home with me and won't be back today or ever. I watched your so called normal children knock the books out of the hands of a handicapped child. I stood and listened as they further tormented him with their vicious rhyme saying that he killed his mother when he was born. I listened to the cries last night of my child who was worrying whether or not he had killed his mommy. If I were to leave him in this classroom, I'd worry that someday he might become like them. Will is so much better than your so called 'normal' children.

Worse yet, he could grow up to be just as cold, heartless, and lacking in compassion as you are Madam, if I were to leave him here. So you can take him off your school roll effective immediately."

Sheep was a man of his word and he decided that he could do a better job of teaching Will how to be a good man than a heartless and uncaring teacher who saw nothing wrong in a defenseless little boy being tormented by his sadistic classmates.

So, Will grew up under his father's loving care learning his lessons from the Bible. He was considered by the other kids and many of their parents as the town fool, but he was a very special young man in the eyes of his father and their Heavenly Father. He developed a love for the Word of God and even at seventeen, he had a childlike innocence and total faith that God could do anything. Others continued to laugh and mock Will, but it mattered nothing to him.

CHAPTER THREE
THE MCPHERSONS

Every small town seems to have a family like the McPhersons. They are the people that you don't want to know when you're going to be away from home for a long and predictable period of time. You just might come back to find that there are no more chickens in your chicken house. The patriarch of the McPherson Clan was Shane McPherson. There is no polite way to describe him. The truth of the matter is that he was a mean drunk. He was a man with a loud and vulgar mouth who talked more than he should, especially when alcohol loosened his tongue. Of course that would have been almost every waking hour of his existence. His family went without necessities most of the time, but Shane's whiskey jug always seemed to have no bottom to it. He was an ignorant man without the wisdom to keep his ill conceived thoughts to himself. He frequently verbally and physically abused both his wife and his children. They often hid in the cornfields for hours at a time after he would come home in order to stay out of the grasp of his enormous hands. They all knew that sooner or later he would pass out from consuming too much alcohol. It mattered little that America had been under the Prohibition for more than a decade. It didn't matter what the law said, Shane McPherson had no trouble locating or consuming large quantities of alcohol on a daily basis.

The matriarch of the McPherson brood was a quiet lady who didn't seem to belong in such a family. Her name was Annie McPherson. Annie was more than twenty years younger than Shane, but dressed like the older ladies of her day. She wore high cut black shoes with metal buttons on them. She also wore long dark dresses and in the summertime, she was never seen without her sun bonnet. She was in fact seldom seen or heard by any of her neighbors. Shane didn't allow her to socialize and when she did feel so lonely that she had no choice but to come out of her house, she was fearful knowing that she needed to get home before Shane found her missing. She was more like his slave than his wife. He often told her how stupid she was. The truth is, Annie was bright enough, she was just illiterate. Her own daddy was also a mean drunk. He saw no need for a girl to have an education and had been almost as verbally and physically abusive to her as Shane. When she eloped with Shane as a teenager, she thought she was fleeing to a better life. Sadly it was a case of, as the old saying goes, "jumping from the frying pan and into the fire".

Annie had come to Sheep on two occasions. Both times she begged him to drop shoplifting charges against her twin boys. Even knowing how they had abused his own son and having presented him with an opportunity to get revenge, Sheep had too kind of a heart to pursue the matters after having heard the apologies of their mother and seeing the sincerity of her tears streaming down her face. Annie couldn't look you in the eye when she spoke with you. I guess she felt so beneath everyone around her. It was the fruit of being constantly berated on a daily basis.

Then there were the twins, Liam and Ian. Liam was the leader and Ian was the follower. It was Liam who was bombed by the pigeon. Whatever Liam could think up to do, Ian was always glad to become his co-conspirator. They were both admirers of their dad and were well on their way to becoming just like him. They too treated their mom like a servant, ordering her around and criticizing everything that she did. Many times Annie had thought about throwing one end of a rope over one of the barn rafters and tying it off and placing the other end in a loop around her neck and jumping from the hay loft. One day she even had the rope in her hand, but when she heard one of her boys outside the barn, trip, fall, and cry out in pain, she instinctively jumped down and ran to help him.

CHAPTER FOUR
THE DREADED
CONVERSATION

It had been nearly two weeks since Doc Grant's visit. It was a slow afternoon at the store and Sheep decided that now was the time that he needed to tell Will the devastating news.

"Will, Buddy. I have something I need to tell you."

"What is it Daddy?"

"Uh, well, you see I need you to keep an eye on the store for me for a couple minutes. I need to step outside for a bit."

Something, seemed off to Will, so he stood back and watched as his dad made his way out back and stood in front of the big white cross with the name Mary engraved on it that stood between the garden and the orchard underneath the maple tree. He watched as his dad fell to his knees in front of the grave then fell flat on his face. His shoulders were shaking slightly as if his dad was sobbing.

Will had always been a dutiful son and did whatever his dad asked him to do, but something seemed terribly wrong and he just had to hear what his dad was sharing with his mom. Quietly, Will slipped out of the house and stood within earshot of his dad without him knowing that he was there.

"Mary, I'm just a big coward. I just couldn't do it. I couldn't tell Will. I made up my mind not to put it off any longer, but I just couldn't get the words out. I chickened out, Mary. How can I tell that poor boy with all he's been through that his father is dying? To make matters worse Mary, word of my condition has spread in the community and it seems that everyone except for Will knows. There are already cruel tongues just a waggin' that are saying that Will needs to be put away in a state home. Mary, those places are bad enough in regular times, but with the Depression all around us and no money in the public treasury, he could starve to death in there. Of course Doc says that he will fight tooth and toenail to keep him out of such a place, but that heathen, McPherson, is running his trap about him not being fit to live among normal people, as if he is anything close to normal himself. It's just a mess and not getting any better. I love Will with all my heart, I just don't know how to tell him. Oh, please Jesus, help me to tell Will."

"He just did, Daddy."

Sheep scrambled to his feet and Will fell into his arms. "Oh son, I didn't want you to hear this like that."

"It's okay Daddy. I'm almost a grown man and with God's help I can make it through anything. Are you in pain? Is there anything I can do for you?"

"No Son, I really don't feel all that bad. My heart has just gotten too weak to keep on beating much longer. I'm tired a lot and short of breath, but I'm not in a lot of pain. Doc says that there is not anything any of us can do."

"I wish the church wasn't boarded up, Daddy. I wish we could go there and pray together. I always felt so close to God there."

"Son, I've got a crowbar. If you think you can use your good arm to pry off the boards, we'll go there, if that's what you want to do, then that's what we'll do."

"I can do it, Daddy."

"Let's go then."

As soon as Sheep could get someone to watch the store for him, he and Will headed out to remove the boards from the church.

Pastor Wiggins had held out for as long as he could, but when the bank repossessed the church parsonage and his wife and children had no place to live, the good pastor said that a man who didn't provide for his own family was worse than an infidel. The church had been temporarily closed in 1930. In the last two years, the town had had no gospel light in it except for the testimony of those whose lights had not been extinguished with the lights of the church.

A layer of dust from the parched land lay all over every surface inside the church. There had not been a drop of rain in that community for more than a year. Sheep said that it was God's judgment for the ungodly lives people were living throughout the 1920's. Politicians were corrupted by gangsters' dollars and senseless violence erupted in towns across the country over territory to sell illegal alcohol. Sheep said that his country had turned away from God's ways and just as He had withheld the rain during the rule of the wicked Ahab and

Jezebel, he was withholding the rain from America.

Sheep and Will knelt at the altar. Will began to pray aloud:

"Heavenly Father, I come to you knowing that you are God and that you are far smarter than either Daddy or me. My heart is breaking. I never got to know Mommy, but Daddy tells me that she was a fine Christian lady who got him to go to church. Please Heavenly Father, don't take my daddy from me just now. I'd miss him terribly if he weren't around. Doctor Grant says that nothing can be done for Daddy, but dear God, I know that nothing is impossible for you. I'm asking you for a miracle. I know that it might be wrong of me to ask a sign of you, but it would sure ease my mind a lot if you could show me something so that I know that you will spare Daddy's life. I wouldn't dare come to you in my own strength, so I come to you to ask these things in the name of your Son, Jesus Christ. Thank you for being here with us and loving us so much. Amen."

Sheep said, "Amen" too and the father and son got up from the altar and began to look around the room.

It was Will who spotted the large church Bible still opened on the pulpit right where Pastor Wiggins had preached his last sermon. He went over and looked at the Bible and it was opened to the following passage of Scripture:

"Daddy, read what it's opened to."

Sheep then began to read.

(Isa 58:6) *Is* not this the fast that I have chosen? to loose the bands of wickedness, to undo the heavy burdens, and to let the oppressed go free, and that ye break every yoke?

(Isa 58:7) *Is it* not to deal thy bread to the hungry, and that thou bring the poor that are cast out to thy house? when thou seest the naked, that thou cover him; and that thou hide not thyself from thine own flesh?

(Isa 58:8) Then shall thy light break forth as the morning, and thine health shall spring forth speedily: and thy righteousness shall go before thee; the glory of the LORD shall be thy rereward.

(Isa 58:9) Then shalt thou call, and the LORD shall answer; thou shalt cry, and he shall say, Here I *am*. If thou take away from the midst of thee the yoke, the putting forth of the finger, and speaking vanity;

(Isa 58:10) And *if* thou draw out thy soul to the hungry, and satisfy the afflicted soul; then shall thy light rise in obscurity, and thy darkness *be* as the noonday:

(Isa 58:11) And the LORD shall guide thee continually, and satisfy thy soul in drought, and make fat thy bones: and thou shalt be like a watered garden, and like a spring of water, whose waters fail not.

"Oh Daddy, right there was my sign. It is God's promise right from the Bible. Daddy remember how you gave food to people from the store who were hungry and you even remarked that you doubted you'd ever see a penny of it paid back. Daddy, I saw you give clothes away out of the store to poor people. Remember the man who was going to go try and get a job, but didn't have a shirt to wear that wasn't full of holes. Daddy you gave him a shirt to try to help him get a job. Daddy, remember the family that was stranded passing through Andrews Crossing on their way out west to find work with no money for gas for their car. Daddy, you let them sleep in the store that night and you filled their tank with gas. Daddy, you're kind and good to others and always close the store on Sundays and even with the church doors closed, you and me still worship the Lord. You are that man God is telling about and it says that your health is going to spring forth speedily. It also said that you would be satisfied in the drought. Daddy, that's talking about you. Don't you see we are in a drought and you need your health to spring forth and you've done everything that God says to do to get His blessing. Daddy, I know that God keeps his promises."

"Son, I know that sounds a lot like our circumstances, but I don't want you to get any false hopes, I'm awfully sick you know."

"But Daddy, we have an awfully big God and now I know He's going to heal you."

CHAPTER FIVE
THE VISION

As strong as Will's faith was, he was still a human being and began second guessing the Scripture that he heard read by his father at church and whether or not it reallly meant what he believed it meant. It sure had fit his father and he knew that the promises of God were sure. He also knew that he could take any care or problem to Jesus. So, he slipped out of his bed and down on his knees and prayed earnestly to Jesus.

"Dear Lord, I know that I should have faith and trust you. I'm weak right now because so many doubts and fears are flooding my mind. I'm sorry I'm this way, but I think it is better if I just come to you and tell you how I'm feeling. Please heal my daddy like you did for people when you walked down here with us. I know you're here with me right now. Please show me plainly what I should do. Thank you for everything, Amen."

It had been a hard and stressful day and

Will's head went to the side and he entered a
deep state of sleep. When he awakened he
had seen a vision in his sleep that seemed so
real it was hard for him to imagine he had
dreamed it. He was in his front yard digging
a hole. At first it scared him because he
thought he was going to have to dig his
daddy a grave, but he reasoned that if his
daddy died he would bury him next to his
mommy and not out in front of the grocery.
He was digging ferociously and all the while
he was digging many of the people were
standing around laughing at him and
pointing their fingers at him and saying all
kinds of mean things to him.
"Lord, I don't understand, I'm even more
confused."
He went to his Bible and set it on its side and
let the pages fall open.
"Lord, I just want you to know that if you
say to me that I should dig a hole out front of
the store, even though I have only one good
arm and hand and the earth is baked solid
from the heat and dryness, I will dig a hole
for you, Lord. I'd do anything to save my
daddy's life. I don't care how many people
might laugh at me and make fun of me, I'll

do whatever you show me to do. I'm hoping
that you will show me why I need to dig a
big hole out there, but even if you don't, I'll
do it by faith."
He then began reading and as he read a huge
smile lit up his face. He laid his Bible down
and rushed to his dad's bedroom door. He
knocked on it.
"That you, Will?"
"Yes, Daddy."
"Come on in."
      Will couldn't wait to tell his daddy the
good news. "Oh Daddy, I had a vision from
God and you're not going to die nearly as
soon as they say. I now know exactly what
to do and how God is going to heal you. He's
going to use me to do it too! We're going to
be doubted and laughed at, but God is going
to work a special miracle just for you,
Daddy."
"Son, are you sure? Are you feeling okay?"
"I've never felt better in all my life, Daddy. I
prayed that God make his will plain to me. I
fell asleep and had a dream unlike any other
one I've ever had. I was digging a big hole
out front of the store. It was hard work
digging that hole and it was made harder by

all the people standing around pointing at me and making fun of what I was doing. Still, I kept on digging moving tiny bits of dirt at a time. I first panicked thinking I was digging your grave, but I figured if I was burying you it would be next to Mommy and not out front. Then I stood my Bible on its side and let it fall open and read where it opened to. Here's what it said, Daddy."

(Joh 5:1) After this there was a feast of the Jews; and Jesus went up to Jerusalem.

(Joh 5:2) Now there is at Jerusalem by the sheep *market* a pool, which is called in the Hebrew tongue Bethesda, having five porches.

(Joh 5:3) In these lay a great multitude of impotent folk, of blind, halt, withered, waiting for the moving of the water.

(Joh 5:4) For an angel went down at a certain season into the pool, and troubled the water: whosoever then first after the troubling of the water stepped in was made whole of whatsoever disease he had.

Daddy, don't you see? We live in Jerusalem Township, and Sheep's Market is here too, and there are five porches just like in the story. You didn't build the store with five porches because of this story did you, Daddy?"

"Well no, I didn't. It just came about as I added living quarters to both ends of the store."

"Daddy, this can't all be coincidence. Think about it! Jerusalem, Sheep's market, five porches, it's all too perfect. I had a vision of digging a hole in the front yard as having something to do with your healing before my Bible fell open to this Scripture. Daddy, if I build this pool, God will send his angel to trouble the water and when you get into the water, you will be healed."

"Son, even if you manage to dig a really big hole, it might not turn into a pool. You do realize that it hasn't rained here in more than a year."

"I know, Daddy, but I trust that if I dig the hole, then God will supply the water."

CHAPTER SIX
THE WORK BEGINS

There was so little to do at Andrews Crossing that the sight of a handicapped young man trying to dig a hole in his front yard was bound to draw a crowd of curious onlookers.

"What's that fool think he's doin' anyway?"
"I don't know, someone said he's got the addle brain idea that somehow diggin' that hole is goin' to save Sheep's life. He's dyin' you know."
"Poor ol' Sheep, it's bad enough for him to be dyin'. He don't need that half-witted son of his embarrassin' him like this. That boy ought to be locked away."
"That's just what Shane was sayin' the other night. We were polishin' off a jug together, and he says we all ought to get up a petition for the sheriff and have that boy committed to the state hospital for retarded kids."

Although he could hear every cruel and ignorant word that they were saying, nothing dissuaded Will from the task at hand. Anyone with a heart should have been moved by his efforts. It was not easy for him to dig in the baked ground having only one functional hand and arm.

"Hey, look Ian. Have you ever seen anyone dig any slower?"

"I sure haven't. If that hair brained idea of his actually did work, it wouldn't save his daddy's life; Liam, Ol' Sheep will be dead of old age before his little lamb ever gets that hole dug!"

About that time for the first time in anyone's memory Annie McPherson spoke loudly and spoke her mind.

"Liam, Ian, I'm ashamed of you both! What has that poor boy ever done to you to make you torment him so? You should get your lazy behinds over there and help him dig instead of sayin' a bunch of mean things to him. Don't you remember that his daddy could have had both of you carted off to the county jail on more than one occasion and was kind enough to give you another chance? Is this how you repay his kindness?"

"Oh shut up woman. You're too stupid to have an opinion on the matter. Nobody wants to hear your two cents worth."

Although the words came out of Liam's sassy teenage mouth, they weren't original. She had heard those same heartbreaking words hundreds of times before from Shane. "I'm ashamed to call you my sons. If you won't do the right thing by this young man, then I will."

There was a shovel not being used leaning up against the store. She grabbed it and pitched in helping Will to dig."
"We're tellin' Dad."
"You go right ahead and do that!"

When a couple of the younger kids that the McPherson twins regularly bullied at school saw Annie McPherson stand up to her sons and pitch in and help Will, they both ran home and grabbed shovels too. They ran back and pitched in. The scene had gotten even stranger. There was a crippled teen, a lady in her long dress and sun bonnet, and two small children working feverishly digging in the baked dirt in front of Sheep's Market.

There was a sound almost like a bull bellowing coming down the road. It was Shane McPherson flanked by his two loathsome sons. He was cursing at the top of his lungs and the words that he was saying was so foul and vulgar that one lady held her hands over her child's ears as they watched the digging. Shane walked up to Annie and got right in her face.

"Woman, you get up out of that hole right this minute and get your bony behind home or else."

Annie for the first time in her life raised her head up and stared Shane right in his eyes and asked, "Or else, what?"

Shane bellowed back, "Or else I'll take you home and beat the ever livin' snot out of you, Woman!"

"Well let me tell you what I know. I know for a fact that you are mean and worthless enough to beat the snot out of me because Lord knows that you've done it more times than I can count, but what you don't know is I'm just plain tired of it. You might manage to do it one more time, but what you probably are too stupid to know is that sooner or later you'll have to go to sleep, and if you beat the snot out of me again, then when you do go to sleep, I'll grab that big iron skillet off the stove that I make your cornbread in and once I've got it heated up to white hot, I'm goin' to beat your head in with it and you won't ever touch me again. You see, this poor little boy here is tryin' to save his daddy's life. I don't pretend to understand how he intends to do it, but I care enough to help a neighbor in need. Me on the other hand, I'm down here diggin' this hole because I figured I needed the practice in how to dig a grave, cause if you touch me one more time you're goin' to need one. Are you too stupid to understand all of that, or do I need to run that past you one more time?"

Shane turned white as a ghost and started stammerin'. Come on boys, I need out of here. I need a drink"

Shane and his boys soon parted ways. Shane had his drink all that afternoon and night. He never got a chance to beat the snot out of Annie. He got so drunk that he fell off of his horse on his way home and in a freak accident landed on his head breaking his neck. He was found a couple days later along the side of an isolated road by his boys, only after the buzzards had found him first.

CHAPTER SEVEN
A HOLE IN THE GROUND

It took several days, but the unlikely team of workers finished digging the hole to Will's satisfaction. Somehow, he just knew what it should look like when it was finished. To the bystanders wagging their tongues, it just looked like a hole in the ground. To Will, it looked like a miracle just waiting to happen.

"Will, what is it? It just looks like a hole in the ground."

"Why that is a pool of water. I call it New Bethesda."

"Now we know you're crazy, that ain't no pool of water. That hole is dry as a bone."

"God ain't finished with it yet. I've done my part, now God will do His. Listen carefully everyone, I hear the sound of an abundance of rain."

Based upon one of Will's heroes, he did as Elijah did. He bowed his head and prayed for rain. In the distant western sky a cloud started forming about the size of a man's hand. The wind started blowing and the tiny cloud kept expanding. The sky became dark and there was the sight of lightening and the sound of rolling thunder. For the first time in more than a year, rain began falling on Andrews Crossing. The voices from the crowd had changed.

"What's happening here?"

"It's raining, praise God it's raining. Yipee!"

The crowd was ecstatic.

"Maybe that boy ain't as weird as we thought."

"I was just thinking that!"

"Yeah, we were all laughin' at him and puttin' him down, but he said one little prayer and for the first time in over a year, it's finally raining."

"I think that young man is special in ways that we can't even imagine."

"I'm inclined to agree with you there."

At first the hole in the ground was just a mud puddle. The rain poured down for two days and when the sun finally came out, the pool was filled with water.

"Hey Will, when is your dad goin' to get healed?"

"I really don't know. We have to wait."

"What are we waitin' on?"

"I'm waiting on God to send his angel down

to stir the water. According to the Bible, the first person to step down into the water after the angel stirs the water will be healed of whatever disease he has. I'm waiting on a miracle from God."

Having found their father dead, the McPherson twins had turned to the only comfort they knew to seek, they opened their dad's jug of whiskey and drank until it didn't hurt so much. Liam was very much like his dad, he too was a mean drunk and was just aching to find someone to take out his emotions on. He wanted to make someone else hurt just as much as he was hurting. Will was standing there at that moment right in front of him and being the natural born bully that he was, he wasted no time trying to make Will miserable.

"So, you're waitin' on a miracle are you? I guess maybe God is goin' to send you down some big ol' angel to make things all better. I got news for you Lambie Pie, there ain't no God and your daddy's goin' to die and if there does happen to be a God, then He don't give a crap about you or me or anyone else in this God forsaken town."

"That's where you're wrong, Liam. God so

loved the world that He gave His only begotten Son, that whosoever believeth in Him should not perish, but have everlasting life. God loves even you Liam as cantankerous and mean as you are. He doesn't love all the bad stuff you do, but Jesus died just as much for you as he did for me. He loves you Liam, and he loves me."
"Oh listen to the Sunday school boy quote those Scriptures. I've got one question for you then, If God loved you so much why would he take your mommy away from you when you were born, and give you a deformed hand, and make it look like you're some idiot every time you try to walk somewhere. Answer me that!"
"Liam, don't you think that I've asked myself that same question time after time? The only truthful answer I can give you is, I don't know. I know that there was a blind man who was born blind and had to spend his life begging, and when Jesus was asked if it was his sin or his parents' sin that caused him to be that way, Jesus said it was neither, he was made that way to glorify God, then Jesus healed him and he did in fact glorify God the same as all the people that saw it or

heard about it. I still trust that God is good and kind and that whatever he allows bad to come into my life, he will turn it to good and it will benefit both me and Him. I believe that with my whole heart. That's the only way that I can be the way I am and still be happy."

About then a shabbily dressed man with several days of beard stubble emerged from the crowd next to the pool to see what was happening. Liam pointed at him and began to torment Will some more.
"Oh look folks, there's a stranger in town. When was the last time we saw one of them? Why that must be Will's angel right there. Just look at him. Hey mister, help me out here, jump into that pool of water and stir it up good. That crippled up boy over there has been expectin' you!"

The stranger who looked like a bum was all too willing to go along with Liam. He jumped right into the pool that Will and his friends had made. He then reached into his pocket and pulled out what looked like a pure gold flask and poured its contents into the pool.
"Way to go mister! Was that whiskey or

folks could it be that was some kind of holy water from the river of life?"

Just at that moment the scraggly man turned to Will and winked his eye and mouthed the words, "Get your dad". He then began to stir the crystal clear water that he had poured into the pool vigorously mixing it with the muddy pool water, turning all the water in the pool into sparkling clear water.

Liam then bellowed out, "Get ready folks we're goin' to see a miracle today."

Will excitedly yelled to his dad, "Daddy come quick, get into the pool, this is the real thing!"

Just then Ian grabbed Liam's arm and yelled at him, "No Liam, don't do it brother!" Liam sneered at his brother and then jerked away and before anyone could stop him, he pushed Will with all his might into the pool. Will fell face first into the water and thrashed about momentarily as you would expect someone with cerebral palsy to do. He then emerged from the water with bounding power. His crippled arm and hand were no longer crippled and he spoke with perfect enunciation.

Being the coward he was, Liam fled

away from Will, who now appeared strong, muscular, and totally able to thrash him properly. Nobody knows to this day what became of Liam after that, he never returned to Andrews Crossing. Whether he too fell off his horse and broke his neck and got eaten by the buzzards or whether he saw that God was real and straightened out his life, but remained too ashamed to ever come home, only God knows.

As Will climbed out of the pool, it reverted back to muddy water. All the healing power had been used up on Will's healing. Sheep's heart was still as weak as it had been, albeit it was filled to overflowing with pure joy, seeing his son healthy and whole. Will then overcome with sorrow sat down on a nearby rock, put his face in his hands and cried.

"I never wanted the pool for my own healing. I wanted to save you from dying, Daddy."

CHAPTER EIGHT
WILL'S FIRST SERMON

In the days following Will's healing, a lot of changes started taking place. Will had spent his life in the store, but because of his handicap he had never been a big help. He could now handle the heaviest stock and communicate with the customers effectively. He made sure that Sheep got plenty of rest and that he did nothing that might put undue stress on his heart. He wanted to buy them as much time together as possible.

A spiritual revival of sorts began to take place as well in tiny Andrews Crossing. You don't witness a crippled boy walk into a pool of water and then a few seconds later walk back out of it totally healed and not be moved by the experience. Two of the most negative voices in the community had also now been silenced with the death of Shane and the disappearance of Liam. The whole community had a much more positive feel to it despite the bleak times they were living through.

When Will had sat crying after he realized that he had received the healing meant for his father, he had felt a hand on his shoulder. He looked up to see Ian standing there.

"For what its worth, I really did try to stop Liam. I am sorry that your daddy didn't get healed the way you wanted. My mom said I ought to tell you I'm sorry for all Liam and me put you through. Just so you know, this is one time I didn't talk back to her. I really did want to tell you that, I guess I just needed a little nudge in the right direction to get the words out. Will, I'm asking you to forgive me for bein' such a louse to you, because right now I'm feelin' like a big piece of nothin'. I never did feel like I was worth all that much. I reckon that was part of what was makin' me act so mean towards you. I really am sorry for it. Maybe some day if you were ever willin', we could actually be friends."

"I think today might be a pretty good day for that, what do you think Ian?"

"That sounds awful good to me. Liam ain't goin' to like it none too much when he gets back, but I really don't care. Carin' 'bout what he thought was always getting' me into some trouble or another. I wanted to ask you 'bout somethin' else. There was somethin' you said to Liam that made goosebumps come up on my arms 'though it seemed to go right over Liam's head. You told him that God loved him even as bad as he'd been. You reckon God loves me too, even bein' a no good McPherson and all?"

"I reckon He sure does."

"I sure wish that preacher man was still around and the church wasn't all boarded up. If that's the case, I'd like to get me some learnin' 'bout God."

"I'd be glad to tell you what I know."

"I'd like that, Will, but the way I see it with things bein' the way they are 'round here, there's a whole lot more people that need it than just me. Could you teach us all the things you know 'bout God down at the church house? I know that people would come from all 'round to hear you, once word of what happened here today spreads from one neighbor to the next."

"Let me talk to Daddy about that. I think I'd like to do that. Maybe that's the answer to the question I've asked God all my life, why I was born the way I was."

"Well, if you do decide to open up the

church house and tell us all 'bout God, let me know, Mom and me will both be there."

That very next Sunday Will found himself standing behind the pulpit. The electricity was still turned off at the church, but they managed with a kerosene lamp to supplement the natural light streaming through the windows. Ian's word was good, He and Annie were both there and Ian was right about people wanting to hear what Will had to say. Every seat in the church was taken and several men were standing on the church's porch with the doors open so as to see and hear Will at a distance.

Will began to speak, "I'd just like to start off by saying that there is nothing special about me. What you all saw wasn't about me. It was about God and His power and His ability to help us even when it seems that we are in an impossible situation.

Sometimes even when God shows up, things don't go according to our plans. We just have to trust in His goodness and grace and mercy even when there are things we don't fully understand. I came to the conclusion that God is smarter than me.

Now many of you used to think that I

wasn't all that bright. The truth is that I had about the same mental abilities before I went into that pool of water as I do now, I just had a lot of trouble saying what was on my mind or acting on the things I thought to do. Let me say up front that I'm no Pastor Wiggins. I don't have the knowledge that that man had, but I do know my Jesus. My walk with God came about when I was just a child, because I responded to love. The truth is you don't have to be all that smart to respond to love. If you have an old dog that you love, I'll guarantee he'll know it and wag his tail and be happy every single time he sees you without fail. I believe that once someone has told you about the love of God, if you respond to it and accept it and not reject it, then you'll never be the same.

The trouble is most people think that God is mad at them and they don't want to be around Him or His people, as if God is going to throw some lightening bolt or something equally bad their direction. Well, I don't guess we got that from a stranger. When Adam and Eve did wrong and ate of that tree that God told them not to eat of, they too went off and tried to hide themselves from God. The wonderful thing about it though is God still loved them enough, in spite of the fact that they had done a very bad thing, that He went looking for them. I stand here today to give you all the good news that God has come looking for you too. So you all might know that I'm not making this stuff up, here is what the Apostle Peter, who was one of Jesus' best friends while he walked here on the earth, had to say about it:

(2Pe 3:9) The Lord is not slack concerning his promise, as some men count slackness; but is longsuffering to us-ward, not willing that any should perish, but that all should come to repentance.

My dear neighbor, that 'all' includes you! It is not an accident that you are hearing these words from my mouth today. It is God's plan for you to hear these words.

Now King David is called a man after God's own heart in the Bible. So he should know a thing or two about God, and he tells us about how God feels towards us human beings in spite of the messes we get ourselves into. Just listen to these words with an open heart.

(Psa 103:1) *A Psalm* **of David.** Bless the LORD, O my soul: and all that is within me, *bless* his holy name.

(Psa 103:2) Bless the LORD, O my soul, and forget not all his benefits:

(Psa 103:3) Who forgiveth all thine iniquities; who healeth all thy diseases;

(Psa 103:4) Who redeemeth thy life from destruction; who crowneth thee with lovingkindness and tender mercies;

(Psa 103:5) Who satisfieth thy mouth with good *things; so that* thy youth is renewed like the eagle's.

(Psa 103:6) The LORD executeth righteousness and judgment for all that are oppressed.

(Psa 103:7) He made known his ways unto Moses, his acts unto the children of Israel.

(Psa 103:8) The LORD *is* merciful and gracious, slow to anger, and plenteous in mercy.

(Psa 103:9) He will not always chide: neither will he keep *his anger* for ever.

(Psa 103:10) He hath not dealt with us after our sins; nor rewarded us according to our iniquities.

(Psa 103:11) For as the heaven is high above the earth, *so* great is his mercy toward them that fear him.

(Psa 103:12) As far as the east is from the west, *so* far hath he removed our transgressions from us.

(Psa 103:13) Like as a father pitieth *his* children, *so* the LORD pitieth them that fear him.

(Psa 103:14) For he knoweth our frame; he remembereth that we *are* dust.

It is right that we should fear and reverence Almighty God, but if you're feeling bad about yourself and you know you've done wrong in His eyes, you should never be afraid to come to God through His Son Jesus. He will remove your sin as far from you as the east is from the west, He will pity you, and He will show you incomprehensible mercy and love. Neighbor, He knows how we're put together and he remembers that we are made from dust. God loves you just the way you are and He wants to adopt you and make you His child and give you a new and better life. He wants to give you a more abundant life better than anything you could possibly ever imagine.

We human beings have a way of trying stubbornly to do everything our way and we always seem to wind up messing everything up. Only when we rest our faith in God's way will we find peace. We didn't get that trait of trying to do it our way from strangers either. When Adam and Eve sinned and ate of the tree of the knowledge of good and evil, their eyes were opened and they discovered that they were running around naked. This new outlook made them feel embarrassed and ashamed. They tried to solve the problem their own way by stitching together some fig leaves to hide their nakedness, but that didn't really work out so great. When God saw their feeble attempts at covering up their shame, He took action. He made coats of skins and made them clothing and covered them properly. Now those little animals that God used to cover their nakedness and shame didn't have zippers in their fur. It took the lives of those innocent animals and the shedding of their blood to cover the sin of a guilty man and woman. God showed a pattern of forgiveness and it was a picture of the innocent dying for the guilty.

As you read beyond Genesis in your Bible you will find throughout the Old Testament that they would bring their animal sacrifices in the manner prescribed by God to pay for that year's sins. There was the shedding of blood and the innocent animals dying and paying the price for the sins of the people.

When you get to the New Testament at the back of your Bible, as time passed, God revealed more of His plan. He tells us that the blood of bulls and goats was not really an acceptable sacrifice, but only a picture of the perfect plan that he brought to man.

From the mouth of John the Baptist we learn that Jesus was the Lamb slain from before the foundations of the world. All of these rituals pointed to God's perfect plan, the coming of Jesus.

All human being inherit their nature to sin against God from their fathers. All the children of men are born sinners. We can't help it. Some may sin less than others, but we all fall short of keeping God's perfect laws. This sin separates us from God and unless this sin problem is addressed and solved, man cannot go to heaven to be with God. Now that is truly a sad picture and a sad state of affairs. The good news we already saw, "God is not willing that any should perish, but that all should come to repentance." Neighbor, God is calling you to Himself this very day and has made a way to remove your sin from you and cleanse you as white as snow.

Here is what God did for you as spoken by none other than Jesus Christ Himself:

(Joh 3:16) For God so loved the world, that he gave his only begotten Son, that whosoever believeth in him should not perish, but have everlasting life.

(Joh 3:17) For God sent not his Son into the world to condemn the world; but that the world through him might be saved.

(Joh 3:18) He that believeth on him is not condemned: but he that believeth not is condemned already, because he hath not believed in the name of the only begotten Son of God.

Jesus was the Son of God. Earlier we said that we get our inherited trait of sin from our fathers, Jesus did not have an earthly father. He was born to the Virgin Mary and the Holy Ghost caused a child to grow within her womb. That child was God in the flesh. In all his life, Jesus never sinned even one time. He is the only man to ever live a sinless life.

The Apostle Paul tells us the price that has to be paid for the sin we do.

(Rom 6:23) For the wages of sin *is* death; but the gift of God *is* eternal life through Jesus Christ our Lord.

Death is the price that has to be paid for sin. Now earlier we said that Jesus never sinned even once in his whole life, so Jesus should never have had to die. Yet we all know the story of how they took Jesus and falsely accused Him and condemned Him to death and crucified Him on a cross. It's easy to see that He did not die for any sin that He did. So why did He die?

The Hebrew prophet Isaiah saw the coming of Jesus, the Messiah, in the future and wrote these words:

(Isa 53:3) He is despised and rejected of men; a man of sorrows, and acquainted with grief: and we hid as it were *our* faces from him; he was despised, and we esteemed him not.

(Isa 53:4) Surely he hath borne our griefs, and carried our sorrows: yet we did esteem him stricken, smitten of God, and afflicted.

(Isa 53:5) But he *was* wounded for our transgressions, *he was* bruised for our iniquities: the chastisement of our peace *was* upon him; and with his stripes we are healed.

(Isa 53:6) All we like sheep have gone astray; we have turned every one to his own way; and the LORD hath laid on him the iniquity of us all.

The sin of us all was laid on Jesus and when He died it was for our sins. He paid the penalty that the law demanded. He made a way for us to be clean and pure in His Father's eyes. When we call out by faith asking Jesus to be our Savior, Jesus wraps us in His goodness and takes away our sin. The Bible tells us that Jesus becomes our high priest and intercedes for us with God much like a defense lawyer in a courtroom. When Satan throws up our sins accusing us to God, Jesus says, 'The penalty for that sin was paid already by me'.

The Bible tells us that when they took the body of Jesus down off the cross that they placed his dead body in a tomb. Three days later, he rose from the dead and is alive forever more, Praise God!

He promises us to do the same for our dead bodies as well. He promises to bring all of his children back to life and we will live with Him forever more.

The Apostle John summed it all up.

(1Jn 5:11) And this is the record, that God hath given to us eternal life, and this life is in his Son.

(1Jn 5:12) He that hath the Son hath life; *and* he that hath not the Son of God hath not life.

Neighbor, it's simple as simple can be. You're a sinner. You needed a Savior to take your place and die to pay for your sins. Jesus volunteered to do that job and he did it perfectly. One man messed up the whole world by sinning and bringing the trait of sin to all the generations that would follow him. The Son of God came and undid the mess he caused, by dying for the sins of the whole world. If you believe this simple story of salvation and call out to Jesus personally trusting Him to be your Savior, he will cleanse you and make you fit for heaven and give you eternal life. If you fail to act on God's gracious offer of forgiveness and cleansing, you will die in your sins and have no other place to go but a devil's hell. I don't want that, God doesn't want that, the angels who will have to throw you into the fire don't want that and will rejoice if you repent and trust Jesus as your Savior, and I can't imagine anyone here in this room preferring a devil's hell to eternal life in heaven. God won't force Himself on anyone. He has given you a will to choose to accept or reject His offer. Please, please, please come forward when I give an invitation and ask Jesus to be your Savior. It isn't about a religious ritual or how fancy your prayer is, it is about a sincere heart wanting to be saved and then after understanding what Jesus gave up to save you, how could you not want to serve Him to the best of your ability?

The Apostle Paul wrote these words:

(Rom 10:8) But what saith it? The word is nigh thee, *even* in thy mouth, and in thy heart: that is, the word of faith, which we preach;

(Rom 10:9) That if thou shalt confess with thy mouth the Lord Jesus, and shalt believe in thine heart that God hath raised him from the dead, thou shalt be saved.

(Rom 10:10) For with the heart man believeth unto righteousness; and with the mouth confession is made unto salvation.

I came to Jesus for his salvation when I was just a little kid. When I was a younger teenager I had some doubts and fears come into my mind and I searched the Scriptures high and low trying to find the exact words to say to be saved. I did not find them. The reason is that God didn't give us magic words, He gave us His Son. If salvation came by repeating words after a preacher, then we could worry that we didn't say them exactly right or we didn't feel the right way or think the right thing when we said them, but when we realize that our salvation depends only on Jesus, then all that matters is if Jesus did everything right. My dear neighbors, we can answer that question with an enthusiastic 'yes'! I believe Jesus did everything right and I'm trusting Him to be my Savior.

I'm sorry I didn't line up a piano player, so if everyone here in a minute or so will sing 'What a Friend we have in Jesus', I'll ask anyone who wants Jesus to be their Savior to simply come forward, pray, and trust Him as their Savior. Please come up and meet me at the altar this morning and don't put it off any longer. Daddy would you lead us in singing?"

"It would be my honor."

Sheep was a little off key as was most of the congregation, but when the invitation was given, Ian was the first to step out of his pew. Annie called out to him, "Wait for me son, I want Jesus too." In all, five people were saved that morning. Several more would follow their lead in the weeks ahead.

God worked a mighty work that day using a young man who was born a cripple and considered the town fool. God has always been able to confound those who profess themselves to be wise with the basest things.

CHAPTER NINE
ABOUT HIS FATHER'S BUSINESS

To Will, it sometimes felt like he had stepped from his life and onto a merry-go-round after his healing. Life was so very different for him and it seemed he was in constant motion. The old board of deacons unanimously voted to reopen the church having heard Will's sermon. The church was bought and paid for and the bank having already repossessed the parsonage left them with nothing in the treasury, but also owing nothing. Will asked no salary, so he was affordable even during the Great Depression. There was no water bill since the bathrooms consisted of two outhouses. Sheep said that he would provide kerosene for the lamps so until things got better, they wouldn't need to turn the electricity on. Mr. Jones who owned a lot of timber land, but had no market for his timber, offered to cut enough wood to keep the stove burning when the fall and winter months arrived.

Will's first order of business was to

visit a pastor a couple towns over that Sheep knew. Will needed a crash course in how to baptize his new converts. He was nervous about doing something wrong and losing someone in the creek. Fortunately, the good pastor had quite a sense of humor and was a good teacher. Will had a King Solomon moment feeling a little too unprepared for the task he found himself pursuing. The pastor gave him a pep talk and a very sincere and humble prayer that encouraged him greatly. Will, like Solomon of old, asked God for wisdom to lead his people. He also prayed that God would grant his prayer and lengthen his daddy's days and give them a lot of time together.

Will was hoping to get back home by dark. It was about a half days journey by horseback each way and the baptism lessons had taken a little longer than Will had counted on. Will was a short fellow and the pastor teaching him was six foot five inches tall. It didn't make for an easy first attempt, but it did give him confidence that if he could baptize that big ol' preacher, then he could baptize anybody. Will had promised the deacons that what he lacked in experience, he would make up for in enthusiasm. Will was amazed at what God had accomplished in the hearts of people who once regarded him as too broken to live among them. Satan had tried to stir animosity in Will's heart for his former critics, but God granted him the wisdom to recognize Satan's devices. His heart was too full of love, compassion, and appreciation for what God had done for him to let bitterness spring up in his heart and cause a division in his revitalized church. He treated everyone at church with respect and love as commanded by his Lord.

Will arrived home safe and sound from his long trip. Sheep asked his son how the day had gone and he said he had stumbled a bit that day, but it had been a good day. He neglected to tell his dad that the stumbling had been in the middle of a creek practicing baptizing a six foot five inch preacher. He and his new preacher friend had already agreed that that was nobody's business.

Will was a bit disappointed when the next Sunday arrived and only about half as many people showed up. The curiosity seekers had their fill, but the faithful continued to come and rejoice. Four more came forward to trust Jesus as their Savior that Sunday and after the services they had a dinner on the grounds with everyone bringing what they could to the meal. After the dinner they went to the creek and Will baptized nine souls, all of whom then joined the church.

Will was determined to fill the church and was determined to bring them in from the highways and hedges. He visited every day in the farmland around town inviting his further out neighbors to come to church in Andrews Crossing. It was four weeks to the day since his healing when he returned home from a productive day of visitation.

He couldn't wait to tell his daddy that he had ran into an old friend of his that Will had never met before and he had agreed to be at church Sunday. As he entered the store he knew immediately that something was wrong. Ian was standing behind the counter and Sheep was nowhere in sight.

"Thank goodness Will, you're back."

"What's wrong Ian?"

"It's your daddy, Will. He's bad, Will. He's real bad. Mom's back there with him tending to him. We've both been prayin' that you'd get back. We come into the store to buy a few supplies and found him passed out behind the counter."

"I shouldn't have left him. I should have stayed closer."

"You can't think like that Will. Your daddy is so proud of you and the job you've been doin' down at the church. He can't stop talkin' 'bout you and how happy he is that God is able to use you the way He is."

"I'm going back to see Daddy."

"I'll keep watchin' the store for you. I'm only sellin' to folks with the money to pay. I tell the others that they will have to wait to talk to Sheep or you."

Thank you Ian. I appreciate your kind words about Daddy being proud of me and your pitching in. You're a true friend. Will wiped the tears from his eyes and put on a brave face before going back into the residence. He didn't want his daddy to see how upset he was.

"How's he doing?"

"Not good Will. We sent for Dr. Grant, but Silas Willard got his leg run over by his wagon and had to have Doc come way out to his place. Your daddy come back out of it for a spell, but he's awfully weak and he can't talk much above a whisper. Honey, if I were you I'd do some tall prayin' and let him rest for now."

"I think I'll do that. Thank you for taking such good care of Daddy. I sure appreciate it."

"Your daddy is a good man. I only wish my sons had had a daddy like that growing up. Your daddy and you too have been very kind to me and my family. It's my pleasure to care for him. I don't know much 'bout prayin' yet, but for what it's worth, I asked the Lord to help him."

"Thank you so much for doing that. He's in God's hands."

"Well, for what it's worth, I reckon that those are the best hands to be in."

"Amen to that."

Will went back out into the store and in

one corner was the farm supplies. Sheep had built a little seat in the corner where Will could go and sit and think or study when he was a boy. The seat wasn't hardly large enough for a nearly grown man, but nevertheless it was Will's special quiet place that he went to whenever life was coming down heavy upon him. In the solitude of that corner, sorrows overcame Will at that moment and the tears began to flow. "Oh God, am I a selfish son? I'd be lying if I didn't say that it has been great to be healed and freed from the body of a cripple and to be able to speak so that everybody can understand me, and to not drool on myself and embarrass myself in front of other people. Lord, my healing was at Daddy's expense. Somehow I can't come to peace with the fact that all this joy that I'm now feeling was at the expense of my daddy who missed out on his own healing. Please Oh my Lord and God have mercy on my daddy and bring him out of this bad spell and please let him stay here with me a little longer. I honestly don't know what I'll do if daddy dies."

Just then Will heard a loud voice inside

the store asking, "Where is everybody?"

"Will got up to see who had come into the store. His heart raced as he rounded the corner and saw who was there. It was the scraggly looking angel who had stirred the water."

"You're back!"

"Yeah, where is everybody? I've never ever had this to happen before. I came to stir the water and there are no people lined up for the blessing."

"I didn't know you were coming back."

"Don't you read your Bible, boy? I came back the same time to Bethesda just as predictable as clockworks for years and I just assumed I would do the same thing here since you went to all the trouble to build the pool and petition the Lord for me to come down to stir the water. Now, here I am and there aren't any sick or blind or crippled people sitting on the porches waiting."

"Sir, my daddy is sick nearly to dying right now. Would you stir the water for him?"

"That's what I'm here to do. Go get your father and if he is the first one in the pool after I stir it, then he will be healed."

"Miss Annie, quick help me get Daddy up and out to the pool. The angel is back."

Remembering what happened the last time, Will worked feverishly to get his daddy on his feet and headed toward the door. Fortunately, Annie was also a very strong farm woman used to doing most of the actual work to be done on the McPherson farm. The two of them had Sheep to the edge of the pool before there was anyone else in sight. The angel poured out his little flask of crystal clear water and again it changed the cloudy water of the pool into crystal clear water. They lifted Sheep down into the water and immediately his ashen white face with a look of death on it turned a healthy pink color. He took a big breath of air and exhaled and bounded back up out of that pool with all the energy and power of a wild stallion. "Praise God, I feel thirty years younger." He then quoted the following Scripture from memory.

"(Isa 40:31) But they that wait upon the LORD shall renew *their* strength; they shall mount up with wings as eagles; they shall run, and not be weary; *and* they shall walk, and not faint."

"Oh Daddy, you're going to be okay."

"Son, I'm going to be more than okay, I feel great!"

As the angel was silently heading away from them, Will called out to him. Thank you, Sir. Will you be coming back?"

"Yes, One o'clock in the afternoon on the day of each new moon."

During one of the worst times in history, God showed up and poured out an unexpected blessing on the insignificant little community of Andrews Crossing. Will led the flock at the little community church there for more than sixty years.

God promises to meet his children's needs, but sometimes he also give them their heart's desire. Annie McPherson had always just longed to be loved and treated with kindness. Over the next two years Sheep and Annie's friendship deepened and turned to love. They were married on Christmas Day, 1934.

Ian and Will became the same kind of

friends that Doc Grant and Sheep had been. They had known each other pretty much all of their lives. Even though in elementary school they had a pretty rocky beginning. When Ian began following the Lord instead of Liam, he became as good a man as the community had ever seen. He made the name, McPherson, something to be proud of, not something to hang your head in shame when you had to repeat it. He was a highly decorated soldier in WWII and exemplified the qualities of those men who were labeled as belonging to the greatest generation.

Although Sheep's market was on the verge of closing in 1932 and Sheep didn't know how he could continue restocking his store, his business survived all the years of the Great Depression. He made an oath to God that he would continue to help the poor in his community and relieve their sufferings by extending credit to all just as long as his supplies held out. God had respect for Sheep's generous spirit at his own expense and like the widow helped by Elijah, Sheep had a flour barrel, a sugar barrel, a cornmeal barrel, and a coffee bin that never seemed to run out. So Sheep just kept helping the poor in his community make it through without starving during the toughest times to ever hit our nation to date. Not once did he ever pressure any of his neighbors to pay their grocery bill. After good times returned though, men gave into his bosom good measure, pressed down, and shaken together, and running over.

Ninety years have come and gone since the angel first stirred the water at Andrews Crossing. Should you ever go on an adventurous road trip and see a sign that says welcome to Jerusalem Township, and come to a cross roads where a funny shaped six sided store stands with a small pool of water out front, my advice is to stop and to wait in one of the rockers on one of the five porches. At one o'clock in the afternoon on the day of the new moon, you may just witness a miracle.

AFTERTHOUGHTS
NOTES FROM THE AUTHOR

The inspiration for this story came from my personal Bible reading. I had just read the account of the man who missed out on healing at the pool of Bethesda, only to be personally healed by Jesus. I thought to myself, what if there was a pool of Bethesda out there someplace in the world today? That was what sparked an idea that I knew I had to turn into a book.

I've always tried to interject a little bit of truth into my fictional stories. When I see someone afflicted with cerebral palsy, I usually think "but for the grace of God there go I". You see I was the one who was born with the umbilical cord wrapped around his neck three times. My mom suffered through thirty-six hours of labor to bring me into the world. When I was born, I was essentially born dead. I was the only one of her five children not to cry upon delivery. The doctor and nurses rushed me out of the delivery room into a nearby room and worked on me to get me to breathe. My mom said it was quite a while before she heard my first cry. My mom also could have died from that labor and I could have died as well or I could have been severely handicapped. I have some mild neurological problems regarding involuntary muscle movements and vocalizations when highly stressed. I keep these symptoms hidden quite effectively and many people who have known me for years are not aware of these problems.

The strangest true portion in this fictional story is the description of the angel. I am convinced that at one point in my life when I was truly at the end of hope, God sent me an angel messenger. I was in a job that I hated going to. I was under thirty years old and on five pills a day to keep down stomach ulcers. No matter how hard I tried, I could never please my management. I was getting ready to leave work for lunch and I said a silent prayer to God telling him how hopeless I felt and how I was at the end of my rope and just didn't know how I could go on much longer. On one wall of my church were written the following words, "Call unto me and I will answer thee and show thee great and mighty things that thou knowest not." I claimed that verse that day in desperation. When I went out the front door to lunch, I nearly ran into this shabbily dressed man with a face full of scraggly whiskers. He had the appearance of a bum. He then spoke to me, "Won't be long now!" I said something like, "Yeah?" Then he repeated the message. "Won't be long now!" He grinned. He went around the corner of the building. I felt compelled to turn around and stop him and ask what he meant. I walked about ten feet to the corner of the building and when I was ready to call out to him, he had disappeared into thin air. The office where I worked had been an old grocery store in the past and was close to a hundred feet deep with no entrance on that side of it, the nearest buildings were several hundred feet away to my left. There is no way even if he was an Olympic runner and broke into a full run after rounding the corner that he could have run out of sight that quickly. Such a task would have been humanly impossible. He simply disappeared when he rounded the corner of the building.

Was he an angel with a message? Add to this experience the fact that two weeks later I had a new job and was moving to a new town. It truly wasn't long after my encounter with him that God answered my prayer I had just prayed and ended my sufferings.

Yes, I am a fiction writer with a healthy imagination and a way with words, but the information in this section is absolute truth.

I would like to clarify my intentions in writing this book. I am not pushing a charismatic approach to the Scriptures. Also, I do not discount the power of God and his ability to help his children in remarkable ways. I still believe that the effectual fervent prayer of a righteous man avails much. God is no less powerful in this present age then he was when the Apostles walked the earth and I do not doubt the literal interpretation of the miracles of healing in the early days of the church. I think this has to be balanced against the fact that the Apostle Paul who had the gift of healing to authenticate his message of the gospel also told Timothy to take a little wine for his stomach's sake and was thankful to God for restoring the health of another dear helper and friend lest he have sorrow upon sorrow. Clearly, he did not have unlimited use of this healing power to heal his friends at will as the church began to grow. I don't believe the story I've told in this book would represent the norm, I would not, however, dismiss it as completely impossible either. With God all things are possible.

In my own family my oldest sister was told that she would never walk again and that she would likely die as a teenager. After five years in a body cast and having survived a surgery that she only had a ten percent chance of surviving, she defied the odds and did walk again and lived to the age of eighty-five. I do not doubt either the power or the goodness of God.

For any reader who has never before heard a clear presentation of the gospel message, I would pray that you will seriously consider the words of young preacher Will and trust Jesus today as your Lord and Savior. Like Will in this story, I trusted Him at an early age and had some doubts and fears later on as a young teenager. I found my peace in recognizing that Jesus did everything right well and I rest comfortably in the knowledge that He will never mess things up for Himself or me. I, like the Apostle Paul, find that there doesn't dwell any good thing in this flesh, but I look to a Savior who will finish the job He started and provide me with a new body that will never sin again and will present me along with the rest of His church as pure, clean, and unreprovable in the sight of God.

I pray that this book will encourage my readers to trust God with the problems they have that are too big to try to solve with their own wisdom. I further pray that you will use whatever talent that you have, or don't believe you have, and step out by faith and serve God to the best of your ability. I hope it inspires my readers to show kindness and compassion to others in time of need and trouble and causes them to trust God to meet all needs when following the will of God. I sincerely hope that you have enjoyed and grown spiritually as a result of reading this small book. Thank you for allowing me to share my heart and thoughts with you. May God bless you all with His abundant and eternal blessings.

The end.